WITHDRAWN from The Free Library of Philadelphia
Book contains theft-detection device that may set off alarm.

W9-AZO-978

Ben,
King of the River

WRITTEN BY

David Gifaldi

ILLUSTRATED BY

Layne Johnson

Albert Whitman & Company
Morton Grove, Illinois

I can't wait!
Our first family camping trip!
I hope Ben doesn't ruin it.

Ben is my brother. He's five . . . and different.
Mom says he has a developmental disability.
He was born that way. He was born with other
problems, too, which is why he's had four operations so far.
Mom says Ben's a fierce fighter. He is. But he also has diaper
blowouts, allergies, and doesn't like new things.

That's why I'm worried.

Dad, Mom, and I pack for the big trip.

Ben spends the time watching his favorite video. He can run a VCR as well as anyone. He loves sing-along videos best. Knows all the words. When his favorite characters and songs appear, he jumps and claps and shivers all over with happiness.

I read Ben his ABC books on the way out of town. When it's time to recite, he gets to G okay. Then skips to L-M-P and Q-R-Z.

"No," I say.

"NO!" he says, throwing the book on the floor.

"Mom, Ben's being difficult," I say.

Ben covers his upper lip with his tongue. Then reaches over to give me a hug.

Even though he's five, Ben still wears diapers. He's working on using the toilet, but he needs practice.

Inside the rest area stall, Ben giggles as Dad tickles his feet and makes grunting noises to get him in the mood. Hearing Dad make bathroom sounds is funny. I have to laugh.

"You got any better ideas?" he asks.

I sure don't.

"Chad!" Ben says, spreading his arms for a hug.

"Gee," I say. "He even has to hug on the toilet."

The campground is great. Much better than the pictures
in the brochure. We pull into site 14, close to the river. "Can we
go for a hike now?" I ask.

Of course we can't. There's a ton of stuff to do first. Mom
cleans the picnic table and sets up lunch while I help Dad with the
tent. Ben's way of helping is to charge inside before the tent is
even up.

"Video," he says before long.

"Campers don't watch videos," Dad says.

I pick up a pine cone. "Look at all these," I say. "You can line them up like racecars."

"No!" he says.

"No, yourself," I say.

I feel like a real trailblazer after lunch when we hike the river trail. My nose goes crazy taking in all the sweet smells coming from the trees and needles and wildflowers. We see a blue heron and two kingfishers. After a while, Ben starts whining and asking for a video.

"Don't you want to go to the waterfall?" I say.

"No," he says.

When a bug flies around his head, he screams, pulling his arms and shoulders in like he does to protect himself.

"It's just a bug," I say.

"Maybe I'd better take him back," Mom says.

"Baby," I say under my breath.

Dad and I hike on till we come to a footbridge that overlooks a waterfall. It has a great name—Wizard Falls. We look hard to figure out why. Then I see it. "Look at the shape of the white water, Dad— up above. A wizard's hat!"

A lady with a dog asks if we'd like a picture together.
Dad gives her his camera. The dog comes right up to me,
jumping up and licking my face.

"You must be a dog-lover," the lady says.

"I'd like to have one," I say.

"Hear that, Dad," she says.

Dad nods, but we both know Ben is allergic to dogs.

Ben is in his swimsuit when we get back. "He's been waiting patiently," Mom says.

Dad and I change and the four of us go to where there's a beach area with people swimming. Ben runs right in up to his knees, then turns around with his arms raised high like he's King of the River.

The water is freezing cold, but Ben doesn't mind. He sits down, water lapping his chest, and plays with the stones and stuff on the bottom. Dad takes a dip and runs, howling, for his towel.

I keep a close eye on Ben. When I come up from a dive I see him blowing bubbles with his face just atop the water. Then he uses his fists to splash himself. "Bang-bang, water-water!" he shouts.

Two boys paddle by on air mattresses. "Look at the weirdo," the boy in purple trunks says.

I check to see if Mom and Dad have heard, but they're busy talking.

Ben's still smacking the water with both hands, splashing and laughing.

The boys fist the water and make snorty laughing sounds to imitate Ben. Then they giggle and paddle off.

PROPERTY OF
GIOVANNI GARCIA

I don't feel much like swimming anymore.

Ben does, though. He stays in till his lips are blue from the cold. When Dad takes him out, he screams "NO!" and starts crying so loud that everyone looks our way.

"Shut up, Ben," I say.

Mom says she doesn't want to hear such talk.

"Then why does he have to be such a baby?" I say.

When Ben takes my hand for the walk back, I pull away, then feel bad and show him how to turn his towel into a cape.

"Batman," he says happily.

"Whatever," I say.

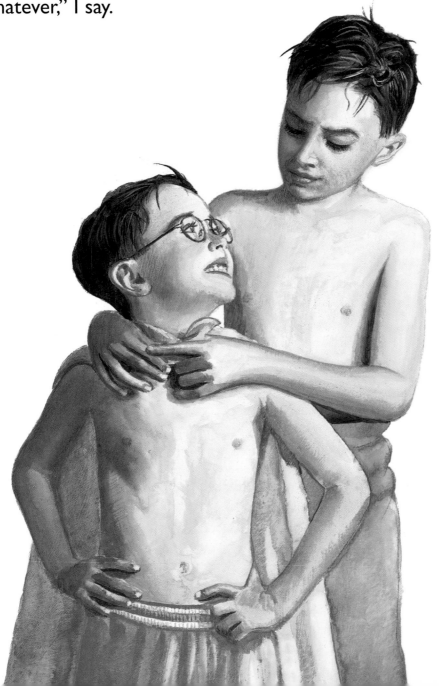

We have macaroni and cheese for supper.

When the sun goes down, Dad lets me start the fire.

"Stay back, Ben," I say.

He claps his hands when the flames take hold.

Mom opens a bag of marshmallows, and I give Ben one of the special roasting sticks I made.

Ben likes his marshmallows to catch fire. They remind him of candles. "Happy Bir-day!" he says. "Mmmm," he says, offering me a blackened treat.

"Thanks, Ben," I say.

"Thanks, Ben," he says, spearing another marshmallow.

Later, Dad and Ben and I take our flashlights and towels to the bathroom.

"Way to go, Ben!" I hear Dad say from inside the stall.

"Ta-dah!" Ben says when the door opens.

"Ta-dah!" I answer.

I walk Ben back to the campsite while Dad washes up. Ben holds onto my arm with one hand and shines his flashlight with the other.

Suddenly there are other beams squiggling the dark. It's the boy with the purple trunks and his friend.

"Hi!" Ben says as if he's known them all his life.

The boys snicker, stopping. "Hi," they say.

I know what they're thinking. My jaw goes tight. I'd like to give them a poke in the nose. "I'm Chad," I say instead. "This is Ben. He's my brother."

Ben spreads out his arms.

"What's that for?" Purple Trunks says.

"He likes to hug people," I say.

The boys move their feet as if trying to free pebbles from between their toes.

"Let's go, Ben," I say. "We've got to put the fire out."

Ben pulls from my grasp, raising his palm out toward Purple Trunks. "Bye, five!" he says.

Purple Trunks looks confused. Then he understands. Grinning, he slaps Ben five.

Ben's smile couldn't get any bigger. He shoves his palm toward the other boy. "Cool," the boy says, giving him five. Ben slaps back a second time—hard—the sound exploding into the dark.

"You staying tomorrow?" Purple Trunks asks as Ben and I start off.

"Yeah," I say, looking back. "If Ben doesn't get allergies or something."

"Maybe we'll see you then," the other boy says.

"Yeah," I say.

Ben and I are supposed to get into our sleeping bags, but decide we need to wrestle first. I'm Wizard of the Falls and Ben is King of the River.

When Mom and Dad crawl into the tent, Ben gives good-night hugs all around.

"Supposed to be even warmer tomorrow," Dad says as we snuggle into our bags.

"I can't wait!" I say.

"King River," Ben says.

"You like camping?" I ask him.

"Camping," he says.

Then Mom flicks off the flashlight, and the night
rushes in to cover us.
Our first camping trip.
Dad, Mom, me, and Ben . . . King of the River.

Note

Hi, my name is Josh Keys. I'm thirteen years old. David Gifaldi, the author of this book, is my uncle. He asked me to write a note about what it's like living with a disabled sibling.

I live with my mom and my eleven-year-old brother, Paul. Paul has a developmental disability. Living with a disabled sibling has its disadvantages and advantages. Sure, lots of people look at Paul, and it's embarrassing. But I just ignore them. It used to hurt a lot when someone would point or laugh at Paul, but now I think, "Who cares what other people think?" Another disadvantage is that my family can't get any pets because Paul has so many allergies. Paul also needs a lot of care. My dad recently passed away, so now it's even harder on my mom. I help out, though.

Let's not forget all the good things about Paul. He is so much fun even my friends like to play with him when they come over. Paul always wants to play and watch movies with me, and he never gets tired. It's funny watching him clap and jump up and down when he watches TV. He is the LOUDEST clapper on Earth! And here's an advantage most people don't know about. Whenever we go to Disneyland, we get a pass to get onto the rides through the exits so we don't have to wait in the long lines. It's so cool!

Overall, I really like having Paul as a brother. And I love him very much.

Tips for living with a disabled brother or sister

- It's okay to be embarrassed when your brother or sister brings you unwanted attention at the mall or in a restaurant. Just remember that your sibling would never knowingly do anything to make you uncomfortable. The best way to deal with stares or rude remarks is to act naturally. Let others see you as you are—a family having fun together. It's likely that the person doing the staring will learn something from what is seen. Something about how healthy families laugh, love, and share with one another.

- Humor is the best policy. What's so horrible about a joyous yell when the food finally arrives at your table? Or when socks are mismatched or shoes are on the wrong feet? Surely there's a smile to be found even in the "perfect timing" of a bathroom accident. As for those new scented markers of yours . . . well, you have to admit they smell pretty good on walls, too!

- Your brother or sister requires a lot of attention from your parents and relatives. You think, "How come he (or she) gets all the attention? Don't I count?" Of course you count! But you can make a sandwich for yourself if you're hungry. You can brush your teeth and comb your hair and do much of your homework on your own. Let your parents know when you're feeling neglected, when it's *you* who needs some special attention. And plan an activity for just you and them.

- You are not a bad person just because you sometimes feel anger or resentment toward your disabled brother or sister. It's healthy to talk about how you're feeling, though. Tell a trusted adult or a friend what's going on, why you're so frustrated, what's been bugging you lately. Many children write or draw their feelings in a journal or diary. You can tell your journal anything, and you'll feel a lot better for it.

- You are not alone. There are Internet sites for kids your age with disabled brothers and sisters. There are support groups, newsletters, workshops, books, and other resources through which children with disabled brothers and sisters get together or speak out and share their experiences. The following Web site offers information and will immediately put you in touch with others:

www.seattlechildrens.org/sibsupp/

You can also type "sibling support" into any search engine to find additional sites.

- Yes, things are more complicated with a disabled brother or sister. But they can also be more rewarding. Think for a moment. Is there anyone who gives you a stronger, more heartfelt *I love you* bear hug than your brother or sister? Probably not!

I am grateful to the following people and organizations for their guidance, suggestions, and information along the way: Mike Brasch, Eileen Laird, Pamela Kende, Donna Keys, Barbara Kouts, JoAnn Simons, Jamie Sorrell, Disability Solutions of Portland, Oregon, and my editor, Abby Levine, who worked tirelessly to "get it right." — D. G.

For Mike, King of the Dads. — D. G.

For Brett and Kevin, with special thanks to
Terri and Keith. — L. J.

Library of Congress Cataloging-in-Publication Data

Gifaldi, David.
Ben, king of the river / by David Gifaldi;
illustrated by Layne Johnson.
p. cm.
Summary: Chad experiences a range of emotions when he goes camping with his parents and his five-year-old mentally disabled brother Ben, who has many developmental problems.
ISBN 0-8075-0635-4 (hardcover)
[1. Brothers — Fiction.
2. Mentally handicapped — Fiction.
3. Camping — Fiction.] I. Johnson, Layne, ill. II. Title.
PZ7.G3625 Be 2001
[Fic] — dc21
00-010522

Text copyright © 2001 by David Gifaldi.
Illustrations copyright © 2001 by Layne Johnson.
Published in 2001 by Albert Whitman & Company,
6340 Oakton Street, Morton Grove, Illinois
60053-2723.
Published simultaneously in Canada by General Publishing, Limited, Toronto. All rights reserved.
No part of this book may be reproduced or transmitted in any form or by any means, electronic or mechanical, including photocopying, recording, or by any information storage and retrieval system, without permission in writing from the publisher.
Printed in the United States of America.
10 9 8 7 6 5 4 3 2 1

The art is rendered in watercolor on gessoed 400-lb. Arches watercolor paper.
The design is by Pamela Kende.

FREE LIBRARY OF PHILADELPHIA

x

3-4   2/02